A WEEKEND WITH Yia Yia

STORY BY: BRIAN BALENO
ILLUSTRATED BY: LISSA SHEAROUSE

ISBN: 9781980931874

ACKNOWLEDGMENTS
I would like to thank the following people:
Irene Baleno (Editor)
Lissa Shearouse (Illustrator)

DEDICATION
To:
My two sons and their Yia Yia (Maria Samolada Ceisel)

Ryan and Jake loved spending weekends with Yia Yia.
Yia Yia is the Greek name for Grandma.
Ryan and Jake's Yia Yia was born in Athens, Greece
but now she lives in the United States.

Yia Yia had a special weekend planned for her grandsons.
Their first stop was the Lincoln Park Zoo.
Ryan and Jake were excited to see their favorite animals.

Ryan wanted to see the elephants.
Elephants are his favorite animal.

Jake likes giraffes.
The zookeeper gave Jake a piece of lettuce
to feed the giraffe.

The last exhibit they visited was the lions.
Lions are Yia Yia's favorite animal.
Ryan and Jake jumped
when the male lion let out a giant roar.

Yia Yia took the boys home for dinner.
Ryan and Jake loved Yia Yia's cooking.

She made them her special Greek chicken and potatoes.
For dessert, they ate baklava with ice cream.

Yia Yia made breakfast for Ryan and Jake on Sunday morning.
Everybody knew Yia Yia at church.
Everyone spoke to her in Greek.

Yia Yia had one more surprise for Ryan and Jake.
She took the boys to the Shedd Aquarium.

Ryan and Jake loved spending weekends
with their Yia Yia.

18

About the Author
Brian lives in Georgia with his wife and two sons.
"A Weekend with Yia Yia"
is his second children's book.

88635373R00015

Made in the USA
Lexington, KY
14 May 2018